A ROCKY MOUNTAIN ROMANCE

JESSICA MEHRING

5 PRINCE PUBLISHING

Published by 5 PRINCE PUBLISHING & BOOKS, LLC

PO Box 865, Arvada, CO 80001

www.5PrinceBooks.com

ISBN digital: 978-1-63112-330-6

ISBN print: 978-1-63112-331-3

Cover Credit: Marianne Nowicki

4282023

THIS TITLE WAS PREVIOUSLY PUBLISHED IN THE 2022 A ROMANCE TO REMEMBER ANTHOLOGY BY 5 PRINCE PUBLISHING

ALSO BY JESSICA MEHRING

A Rocky Mountain Romance

Firewall

A ROCKY MOUNTAIN ROMANCE

HANK

Hank Drummond wasn't a religious man, but he was praying fervently as he got the last signal booster online. "Paul," Hank said into his radio. "You're begging for trouble with this setup."

The radio crackled before a deep voice boomed through, "You're paranoid, Hank. It'll be fine. Get off the line."

Hank sighed as he stood up from his crouched position next to the outlet by the ancient auditorium's front entrance, nearly hitting his head on the edge of a green lacquered "St. Francis Holiday Craft Show" sign. He clipped the radio to his belt and brushed his hands on his jeans. "Your funeral," he mumbled, pushing a drooping lock of hair off his forehead.

A large thud followed by a hissed curse word drew his attention to one of the sets of double doors leading into the auditorium's main floor. A woman with jet black hair styled in a sleek bob was wrestling with several bags, a large box, and a stack of antique books.

Just as Hank stepped forward to help her, someone opened the door from the inside. "Let me help, Miss Green," said a deep voice from the other side of the door. Two large, hairy arms emerged and took several of the woman's items off her hands.

"Thanks. Call me Amity," she said as she walked through, her black boots clicking on the hardwood floor.

Hank stared at the door as it creaked closed and clicked shut.

Justin, Hank's assistant who always seemed to show up only after the work was done, sidled up to Hank. "Hard to believe she's slumming it with us here at the craft show," he said. He looped his thumbs through the belt loops on his khakis and rocked back on his loafered heels.

"What do you mean?" Hank said, crossing his arms.

"She's from New York City. Makes fancy jewelry."

"How'd a woman from New York end up in St. Francis, Colorado?"

Justin shrugged. "Maybe she took a wrong turn in Aspen."

Hank's barking laugh echoed in the foyer between the outside doors and the inside ones. The little old ladies setting up their cash boxes to take visitors' entry fees looked over and glowered. He did a little bow at them. "Ladies."

The old ladies stopped glowering and started giggling.

Hank nodded his head toward the door at the far end of the hall. "Justin, I need you to go make sure all the connections look sound. The wifi signal lights on the routers should be solid green. I'm going to be on the main floor for a bit."

"Aye aye, cap'n," Justin said, putting his hand to his blond head in a mock salute.

Hank gave the ladies a little wink as he walked by their worn plastic card table and through the double doors onto the auditorium floor. The smell of pine, cinnamon, and cider hit his nose. *It's like Christmas exploded in here.*

It was hours yet before the St. Francis Annual Holiday Craft Show opened its doors to the public, but the mess and chaos in the city auditorium made Hank wonder how they'd possibly be ready in time.

Someone shouted his name from across the room, and Hank craned his neck to find the source. A waving hand got his attention, and he weaved his way through the piles of boxes, still-folded card tables, and dismantled plastic Christmas trees toward the frantically waving hand.

"What's the wifi password?" Tricia Bonham asked loudly as he approached her neatly bedecked table. The rest of the city auditorium might look like a disaster area, but Tricia's selection of candles and cards was neatly organized and labeled.

"It's 'francisholiday'," Hank answered, trying to keep the irritation out of his voice. That information had been sent out to all the vendors at least three times by now.

Tricia raked her manicured fingers through her long blonde hair. "Thanks, Hank." Her bubblegum-pink lips stretched into a smile that didn't reach her eyes.

Hank nodded and turned to get back to his job—making sure all the vendors had an internet connection during the show—when Tricia cleared her throat. He turned back. "Yeah?"

"Come by after the show," she said. "I'll buy you a cider for your trouble." Tricia's head cocked to the side, and her blonde hair fell like a curtain over one eye. It was a move that probably came across as seductive to the average male—but Hank knew her type. She was the planning director for the city, and thought she owned the place...and everyone in it.

"We'll see," he answered. "I've got a lot to do today." He didn't wait for her response. He turned on his heel and made a beeline toward the end of the aisle.

In his haste, he ran straight into Amity Green.

HANK SMASHED INTO AMITY AND HE INSTINCTIVELY REACHED OUT to grab her as she fell. Unfortunately, he missed her arm by centimeter. There was a crunching noise as she fell back into an open box of garlands, her butt wedged in the fake pine and tinsel. She looked so ridiculous there in the box, her skin-tight, dark denim pants and pointy black boots dangling over one edge, and her arms flailing in their blood-red sweater over the other edge.

Hank burst out laughing.

"It's so nice that this is entertaining for you," she said in a low voice, "but can you stop laughing for a moment and help me out of this thing?" She reached a hand up.

"I'm so sorry," Hank said, using all his willpower to stop laughing. He reached down and grasped her pale, thin hand, then pulled. She was lighter than he expected, and he pulled harder than he should have. Amity went flying a second time—but this time he caught her.

Amity's cheek pressed up against Hank's chest, and she grabbed his shoulders in both hands to regain her balance. She smelled like jasmine. Her eyes rose to meet his, and he was astonished by their depth. Brown wasn't the right word for them, nor was black. They were chocolate and dark-roast coffee and they threatened to drown him if he kept her gaze.

Hank put his hands on her upper arms and helped Amity right herself. Her porcelain face was inches from his. His breath caught. "You okay?" he whispered as he sank even deeper into those eyes.

Amity looked down, breaking the connection. "I'm fine. Now if you don't mind." Her eyes moved to his hand on her right arm.

Hank pulled his hands back and tucked them into his back pockets. "Can I help you back to your table?" He looked down at the pile around her feet. "Seems like you might have more than you can carry here."

"I was carrying it just fine before you bowled me over," Amity put her hands on her hips. She shook her head and took a deep breath. "You can help me clean it up, though." She crouched down, righted a box, and began scooping what looked like beaded jewelry into it.

Hank got down on his knees next to her, and he breathed in sharply at the pain of the hard floor on his kneecaps. "These are beautiful," he said, picking up one of the beaded creations. It appeared to be a string of delicate crystal beads, with elaborate knotted designs at either end. "What are they?"

"Bookmarks," Amity said, snatching the thing out of his hands and dropping it into her box.

"Huh," Hank grunted.

"What do you mean 'huh'?"

"I heard you were a fancy jewelry designer."

"I *am* a jewelry designer."

"This isn't jewelry."

"Nope."

"But you made them. To sell here at the show?"

"Yep."

"You're not one for conversation, are you?" Hank snorted.

Amity rocked back on her heels and fixed those dark eyes on his face. She took a deep breath before answering. "I'm doing my sister a favor. She's eight months pregnant, so she couldn't handle managing a table this year."

"What does your sister make?"

"Readers," Amity said with a soft laugh. "She owns Booktopia, that little bookshop on Main Street. So she usually sells a selection of books, bookmarks, tote bags, that kind of thing, here at the show every Christmas. Mostly to advertise the bookshop."

"I see," Hank said, rubbing his chin. "So you made bookmarks to sell, to advertise the bookshop."

Amity nodded. "Well, I was also really bored. So I figured it was an opportunity to put my skills to use in this silly little town."

Hank laughed.

Amity blushed. "I'm sorry. That was rude. I just…I moved here from New York City recently, and it's been a hard adjustment."

"I can imagine there was some culture shock involved," he responded. Amity's dark hair swayed as she nodded her response, and Hank couldn't help but notice how the ends of her sleek bob brushed the delicate line of her jaw. *And I'm staring again. Dangit.* He looked away quickly. "Let me help you to your table," he said quickly, reaching for the box.

Amity didn't argue this time. She stood up and began walking back down the aisle Hank had just come from—and he realized she was going in the direction of Tricia Bonham's table. He groaned inwardly.

Luckily, Amity's table was three spots away from Tricia's. The blonde woman still stared at him as he set Amity's box down on the metal folding chair, but she made no move to come talk to him. When he looked up, he realized why. Amity was staring daggers at Tricia.

Hank stepped around the side of the table and placed his body in Amity's sightline. When her eye contact with Tricia was broken, her angry gaze shifted to him. In an instant, the anger faded and she looked at Hank quizzically.

"What's with you and Tricia?" he asked.

"Family drama," Amity replied.

"It looks like you want to take her head off."

She tilted her head and pinched her lips together. "I kind of do."

"Why?"

"Long story."

Hank sighed. "You are a tough nut to crack, Amity Green."

Amity's eyebrows rose. "How do you know my name?"

"People talk. I'm Hank Drummond, by the way." He extended his hand.

"I hate this town." She took his hand in hers, and squeezed firmly.

Hank was surprised at the strength of her handshake. "That's too bad. This town seems to *love* you. You give them all kinds of good stuff to talk about."

"You mean gossip about."

Hank shrugged. "I've lived here for a year, now, and I can

honestly say these are mostly good-hearted people. Sure, they talk—and sure, you can call it gossip—but it's because they care. They care about this town, what goes on in it, and the people who live in it."

"I preferred it in Manhattan where I could be anonymous among millions of people."

"So why are you here?" Hank shifted his weight and hooked a thumb in his back pocket.

"Told you. Long story."

The two stared at each other for a beat before Hank had to avert his gaze. He nodded at the box of bookmarks. "How much?"

"Ten dollars," Amity said with a lopsided smile. Her red lips looked positively edible.

"Ten dollars for a bookmark?" Hank gasped.

"Ten dollars for a handmade, jeweled reading placeholder."

Hank shook his head and pulled his wallet out of his back pocket. "At least it's going to a good cause. Booktopia is my twelve-year-old niece's favorite place to go when she's visiting."

"I'll be sure to pass on the praise to my sister," Amity said, extending her hand to take his card. She pulled her phone out of a small black satin purse on the table, swiped her finger across the screen, and frowned. "Do you know the wifi password? It's 'francisholiday', right?"

"Yeah, that's right." Hank smiled. *Good to know someone reads the emails we send out.*

"I was connected when I got here a half hour ago, but now I'm not." Her red lips reshaped from a frown to a pout.

Hank pinched the bridge of his nose. "Can I see your phone?" He took it from Amity's hand and navigated to the wifi settings. Sure enough, the auditorium network wasn't on the list of available connections. "I've got to go take care of this."

Amity squinted at him.

"I'm the IT manager for the City of St. Francis. That's what

I'm doing here today, making sure the network is set up right so you vendors can take credit cards."

Amity's dark eyes widened. "Go," she said simply. "Wait, hang on." She waved him back, then pulled one of the crystal beaded bookmarks out of the box and tossed it at him.

Hank caught it in one hand. "I'll pay you later."

"Get me good wifi," Amity said. "We'll call it even." She smiled sweetly.

But Hank didn't want to go. He wanted to stay and ask a million questions of this porcelain woman from New York City. Duty called, but his curiosity remained at the table covered in beaded crystal bookmarks.

AMITY

AMITY WAS SURPRISED AT THE SLIGHT DISAPPOINTMENT SHE FELT watching Hank walk away. But she wasn't disappointed in the view. His button-down blue shirt ended at just the right place in the back to show his toned glutes moving underneath his jeans. She shook her head briskly to clear her thoughts.

Stepping around the front of the wobbly folding table, Amity pressed her hand down on either side. Putting folded paper under the left leg seemed to have done the trick to stabilize the wobble when she first arrived, but it was unstable again. She took her purse off the table and put it on the folding chair. Then she reached under the table and adjusted the folded paper under the leg before sliding out two boxes. From the first box, she removed a black cloth, and deftly draped it over the table. From the second box, she pulled out two signs, a small black bust, and a three-tiered jewelry stand. After a few minutes spent fiddling with placements, the table was ready to be bedazzled in her beaded crystal bookmarks.

The third box Amity slid out from under the table was a mess. She had dropped it on the way in, and again when Hank ran into her, and it looked like a shattered chandelier. Amity took a deep breath and dove in, praying the bookmarks weren't too tangled up. She was pleasantly surprised to find that they were easy to separate, and it only took her a few minutes to get them placed artfully around the table.

She stepped back to get a look at her table arrangement. The black, crushed velvet tablecloth gave the folding table a touch of elegance. She chose the fabric because it brought out the shine in the beaded crystal bookmarks, but she had to admit it also made her table stand out in the crowd. Amity adjusted the placement of the two signs on either end of the long table, both advertising the Booktopia bookshop.

"Beautiful," someone said from behind her.

Amity spun around and found her brother-in-law, Mark Parish, standing behind her. His face was rounded in a cherubic smile under his thick glasses, and yet he still managed to look like a scarecrow in his jeans and button-down flannel shirt. "You should send Anne a picture," he said.

"Good idea," Amity said with a grin. She pulled her phone out of her back pocket and noticed the wifi icon was lit up. *Hank must be good at his job. That was fast.*

"Here," Mark said, holding out his hand. "Hand it to me. I'll take a picture of you at the table."

Amity shook her head. "I'm good. Thanks Mark."

"There's no shame in selling your work at a small-town craft fair, you know," he said, frowning.

Amity's heart sank. "No, it's not that." *It's a little bit that.* "I just think we need to post the photos to Booktopia's social media feeds, and the focus should be on Booktopia, not on me."

"You two know more about that stuff than I do," he said with a shrug. "I just stopped by to see how things were going, and to wish you luck. And…to ask that you keep a close eye on Anne. I don't like leaving on a work trip so close to the due date."

"She's a month out," Amity said.

"Our neighbor's son arrived at 32 weeks last year…"

"That's unusual, I think."

"I just worry."

Amity put her hand on her brother-in-law's shoulder. "I know. I've got her, though. I'll keep a close eye, okay?"

Mark's childlike smile returned. "Thanks. I'm so glad you're here."

"Me too," Amity said. It wasn't a total lie.

"I'll be at the Westin in Denver, and I'll drive back Saturday morning. You two call me for anything, okay? If the baby gets the hiccups, I want to hear about it."

"I'm sure you will. That's been driving Anne crazy. She says the tapping feeling is like Chinese water torture."

Mark laughed, a rolling sound that Anne had told Amity was one of the reasons she fell in love with the man five years ago. "I'm going to hit the road. Be good," Mark said. He gave Amity a quick hug before walking back down the aisle and out the auditorium doors.

After taking a few photos of the table, Amity walked around to the back side and flopped down in the metal folding chair. She pulled up Booktopia's Twitter account and began writing a tweet to advertise the shop's presence at the holiday craft show.

Out of the corner of her eye, she saw a familiar blue shirt approach the table.

"Wifi working now?" Hank asked, his green eyes twinkling at her.

"Yes! Thank you." Amity flashed her phone at him. "Just getting ready to put up some social posts for the shop."

Hank shuddered. "Marketing was never my thing. I always preferred to be on the technical side of the house."

"I get it," Amity said. "I let my business partner do all the marketing for my jewelry back in New York." Her stomach did a little flip at the memory. "Turns out it's not always a good idea to let other people hawk your wares."

"I'll take your word for it. I have never had the desire to be

self-employed. I like having a firm start and stop to my workday."
Hank put his hands behind his head and stretched, and Amity
couldn't help but notice the flash of abs.

"Smart man." Amity laughed, leaning back in the chair. "Sad
you don't do any freelancing, though. Booktopia's wifi has been
on the fritz for weeks."

"I can come out and take a look," Hank said, putting his hands
on his hips. His shoulders and upper arms strained the seams of
his shirt.

Heat rose in Amity's cheeks and she fought down the flush—
her pale skin had always revealed her emotions much too readily.
"That would be amazing. Is tomorrow at 5:30 okay? I'll be done
with the show at 4:30."

"And I'll be done at work at 5. That's perfect."

They stared at each other a beat too long for Amity's comfort.

"Great," she said quickly. "See you there."

Hank's smile crinkled the corners of his green eyes. He
nodded, then gave Amity another great view as he walked away.

THE BOOKMARKS FLEW OFF THE PROVERBIAL SHELF. APPARENTLY
being the object of gossip in this town was really good for
business.

"What's it like in New York City?" a sweet young woman with
red hair and vibrant freckles asked, leaning on the table. "I hear
it's loud. And dirty."

"It's loud," Amity said, "but you get used to it. Have you been
to Denver?"

"Yes," the young woman replied. "Of course. It's the only city
that has any culture in this state."

"What does it smell like you to?" Amity stood and tucked her
hands in her front pockets as she moved a little closer to the
woman.

"Like marijuana and urine, mostly." The redhead giggled.

Amity laughed with her. "In my experience, wherever people congregate, there are *people smells*. Manhattan is no different. Maybe just a little more puke smell than marijuana."

"What are you people talking about over here?" Tricia Bonner approached Amity's table with her nose in the air. She pushed her blonde hair behind her ear and scowled.

"Smelly people," Amity said, raising one eyebrow.

Tricia and Amity stared at each other, neither blinking. The redheaded young woman stood awkwardly between them. Only her sudden cough ended the staring contest.

Flinging her long blonde locks over her shoulder, Tricia turned and walked back to her table at the end of the aisle.

"That woman needs a good..." Amity started before realizing she had an audience. The redhead had been joined by two other giggling young women and an older man.

The man walked around the table like he owned the place, and thrust his hand out at Amity. "Carl Northrup," he said, waiting for Amity to take his outstretched hand. He was crisply dressed, with neat salt-and-pepper hair and a golf tan.

"Um, nice to meet you, Carl," Amity said, staring at his hand. She brushed her bangs out of her eyes.

"My wife is a big admirer of your work," he continued without missing a beat. He put his outstretched hand into his sports jacket pocket and pulled out a card. "When she heard you were here, she insisted I come talk to you. I'm over in Aspen for the weekend for a business retreat."

"That's so nice that your wife is a fan. Where is she today?" Amity slid easily into the small-talk after so many years of practice.

"She's home in L.A. We have a line of fine jewelry stores across Southern California. I'd like to talk to you about partnering up."

Amity all but snatched the business card out of his hands.

"My wife showed me some of the pieces she bought from you in New York. They're stunning. When she wears one necklace in particular, it's like she's wearing the stars around her neck." His thin lips stretched into a warm smile.

"That makes me so happy to hear," Amity said, grinning from ear to ear.

"I have to ask, though. Why are you…*here*?" The way he said the last word was like he was talking about a backwoods hick town.

"I wanted to take a break from the scene in New York, and my sister lives here," Amity said. She hurried to add, "St. Francis isn't far from Aspen and Vail, so I don't feel like I'm too out of the loop here. And it's quiet, so I'm able to get some good work done."

Carl looked at the few remaining bookmarks on the table.

"Advertising for my sister's bookshop," Amity said before he could ask.

The man nodded. "Call me after the show tonight. Let's talk." With that, he walked away.

The three young women were still standing at the table, and had clearly been eavesdropping. The redhead piped up, "Oh my gosh! I bet he wants your jewelry for his stores out in California. Are you so excited?"

Hank walked by the table and gave Amity a wave and a warm smile as he passed.

"I think so," Amity said, her eyes following Hank down the aisle. "But with men like that, I never count my chickens." *Because men like that are often wolves in disguise.*

IT DIDN'T TAKE LONG TO PACK UP AMITY'S TABLE AFTER THE ST. Francis Annual Holiday Craft Show ended—there weren't any bookmarks left to pack. They had completely sold out.

With the last of the gear safely stored in the trunk of her little red Audi, it was time to make the call. Amity pulled her phone and Carl's card out of her pocket, slid into the driver's seat, and dialed the number.

"I'm glad you called," Carl said on the other end of the line. His voice reminded her of her late uncle's—a smoker and a drinker until his dying day.

"How'd you know it was me?" Amity asked.

"New York area code."

"Ah."

"I'm going to get to the point. I'm here with several friends for a ski retreat and I'm not supposed to be doing any business, but my wife would divorce me if I came home without a commitment from you. I want you to fly out to L.A. with me on the twenty-fourth."

Amity frowned. "That's in three days. And it's Christmas Eve."

"Is that a problem?"

"I'm not sure…"

"Look, my wife is throwing a fancy holiday party on Christmas Eve, and we want you as the guest of honor. That'll also give us the weekend to show you the new shopfront on Rodeo Ave, and where we'd like to show your work."

Rodeo Ave. Amity tried not to squeal. "I see. I just need to talk to my sister before I can commit to anything."

"I'll call you on Friday at noon while the guys are getting their massages. Give me your answer then." Carl didn't say goodbye before he hung up.

Amity stared at her phone. *Did that just happen?*

HANK

INSIDE THE BOOKTOPIA BOOKSHOP ON MAIN STREET, HANK wound his way through shoulder-high bookshelves and tables covered in book-related trinkets, and followed the sound of shouting. The older man at the register had pointed him toward the back of the shop, but Hank had no doubt he could have found his way to Amity and Anne by the sheer volume of their fighting.

The two women stood face to face at the back of the shop, in front of what Hank assumed was the door to the back room. The door had a bejeweled Christmas tree painted on it, and brass bells hung gaily from the handle. Amity was unmistakable with her black bob and red lipstick. The other woman was easy to identify as Amity's sister, Anne—not only by the personal nature of their fight, but also because they shared the same arched eyebrows and no-nonsense tone.

"That's Christmas Eve!" Anne yelled. "And you don't even know these people."

"I looked them up last night. They're the real deal. Once I saw her picture, I remembered meeting the wife at a couple of shows in New York," Amity argued back.

"This is crazy," Anne hissed.

"This is my ticket to a new life," Amity responded, calmer now.

"You already have a life."

"No, I have a holding pattern."

Both women's eyes snapped up and landed angrily on Hank. He raised his hands in surrender. "Am I interrupting?"

"No," they both said in unison.

Amity was dressed in skin-tight black pants, with a hunter green sweater and black ballet flats. She looked like she stepped out of a Manhattan Christmas catalog. It took just a split second for her expression to shift from annoyance to welcome—and Hank felt relief that he was on the receiving end of the welcome face.

"Hank, thank you so much for coming," she said. She pointed toward the woman next to her. "This is my sister, Anne."

Anne wasn't quite as pale as Amity, and her long, curly hair was a rich chocolate brown as opposed to Amity's straight black bob. Both women stood at the same height, several inches shorter than Hank's six feet, two inches, but not short by any means. Anne also appeared immensely pregnant.

As if his noticing made the baby stir, Anne put her hand on her belly and arched her back. "It's nice to meet you, Hank. But this baby is begging me to get off my feet," she said, sounding a bit out of breath. "Can we have this conversation in my office?"

Amity's brows drew together. "Of course," she said, opening the door with the Christmas tree on it.

What Hank saw on the other side of the threshold was not what he was expecting. On the far end of the room, across from the door, was an ancient looking stone fireplace. A heavy oak desk with a leather wingback chair behind it took up the left side of the room. Two leather club chairs sat in front of the fireplace, with a marble-topped coffee table between them.

Most surprising of all, art covered every inch of the walls. There were classic paintings, hanging metal sculptures, miniature watercolors, and floating shelves lined with pottery. Every kind of art Hank could think of was somewhere on these walls.

"This is...amazing," Hank said, his jaw slack. He ran his hand over his chin as he spun around to see everything.

"Thanks," Anne said, plopping down in the wingback chair and putting her feet up on the desk. "I love art."

"Clearly," he said.

Amity laughed lightly. "Anne and I grew up in the New York art scene. Our mother was a painter and our father was a sculptor. It was quite the family scandal that we didn't become fine artists. I make wearable art, and Anne collects art. We're rebels." Her red lips stretched in a wicked smile.

"I didn't rebel so much as run," Anne said with a laugh. "I ran to Denver, met the love of my life when I was a senior in college there, then we ran to Aspen to become ski bums."

"I take it the ski bum thing didn't work out for you," Hank said as he pulled the club chairs over in front of the desk, one by one. He sat in one and patted the seat of the other for Amity to join him. She obliged, perching lightly like a finch on the heavy chair.

"There's no money in being a bum," Anne replied. "We were ready to settle down, and I'd always dreamed of having a bookstore—in addition to being an art junkie, I'm a total bibliophile. We met the former owners of this place at the lodge in Aspen, and they mentioned they were looking to sell. And here we are." She pulled her feet off the desk and slowly sat up straighter in the chair. "A great little bookstore in a building owned by a guy who thinks plumbing and electricity are luxuries."

"That would be Tricia Bonham's father she's talking about," Amity said through gritted teeth.

"Oohh," Hank said, suddenly a bit clearer on the stare-down at the fair yesterday.

Anne expounded, "Her father pays for just enough repairs on this building to sneak under the city government's urban development radar, but not enough to make it comfortable to run a business here."

"And Tricia acts like she owns this place," Amity added, the corners of her candy-apple lips turning down. "I actually caught her walking out with a stolen book last week. She just batted her eyes at me and said her daddy would take it out of the rent." Her long white fingers curled into a fist on the arm of the club chair.

Anne burst out laughing. "Amity pretty much wrestled Tricia to the ground to get the book back. It was the funniest thing I've ever seen. I thought I was going to go into labor laughing so hard."

Amity smiled at her sister—a genuine, loving smile that Hank knew all too well. His sisters had the same bond. No matter how mad they got at each other, they were still best friends.

Amity clapped her hands together. "Well, let's get down to business. I'm sure Hank doesn't have all night." She turned to face him, tucking her dark hair behind her ear. "Anne and I are in a disagreement over the internet in this place, and you're going to prove me right."

"You mean prove *me* right," Anne argued.

Hank grinned. "How about you tell me what's going on and I'll see if I can help fix it."

"The wifi drops constantly," Amity said. "You can't keep a connection for more than a minute."

"We've tried calling the cable internet company, but they tell us the signal looks solid," Anne followed.

"We've tried three different routers. And we've got extenders plugged in all over the shop," Amity added.

"I think it's the electrical in this crappy old building," Anne said with a sigh.

"And I think it's a setting issue on the router that we just haven't figured out yet," Amity finished.

Hank was getting dizzy looking back and forth between the

two women as they spoke in turn. "Can you point me to the router?" he asked.

Both women pointed to a door on the wall behind him that he hadn't noticed was there. He walked over, opened the door, and felt the wall for a light switch.

"It's a pull string just above your head," Amity said from right next to him.

Hank nearly jumped. He hadn't heard her follow him. She reached over his head and pulled the string to turn on the light. For the second time that week, he was awash in her hypnotic jasmine scent.

The closet was small and packed to the brim, but he quickly located the router on a low shelf. Looking over his shoulder at Amity, who was standing in the doorway behind him now, he said, "It may be boring watching me work. You don't have to wait around in here."

Amity shrugged, her shoulders bumping her long metal chain earrings and making them jingle. "The only thing on my agenda tonight is watching *Murder, She Wrote* reruns," she said.

"I love *Murder, She Wrote!*" Hank said. He hummed the theme song, and Amity joined him.

"You guys are nerds!" Anne shouted from across the room. "The baby has finally stopped kicking my kidneys, so I'm going to get back out front."

Hank heard the office door close, and he was suddenly very aware that he was alone with Amity. She leaned on the closet door and crossed her arms. "Good riddance," she said, smiling. "So, anything I can do to help?"

Out of the corner of his eye, Hank looked at her skin-tight pants. He bit his tongue until he could control what came out of it. "Can you find me a flashlight?" Hank asked after a beat. "The overhead light isn't cutting it."

"Absolutely." Amity left the room, but her perfume remained.

AMITY

"HE'S CUTE," ANNE SAID AS AMITY WALKED UP TO THE REGISTER where she stood.

Amity shook her head and kept walking around the front counter until she stood next to her dear, annoying sister. "Don't start." She bent to look at the shelf underneath the register, then reached her hand all the way to the back of the middle shelf. "Aha!" Amity pulled out a bright pink flashlight. When she stood up again, Anne was leaning against the wall, rubbing her belly. Amity frowned at her.

"Braxton Hicks contractions," Anne answered the unspoken question. "False labor."

"Where's Clyde?" Amity asked, crossing her arms.

"On break."

"You really need to hire more help than just Clyde. One employee is not enough. You can't be the only one working the floor when he goes on break. What if you went into labor?"

"Hire more help with what money?" Anne asked. She looked at her protruding belly, snug in a stretchy floral top. "We're barely doing more than breaking even. What extra we manage to make goes straight into savings for when this little one is born.

There have been a few months we've almost had to sell some of the CDs we invested in. That would have killed me. Those CDs are the only thing keeping my hope alive that eventually we'll be able to buy a proper building for this bookshop."

"I'm sorry," Amity said. She uncrossed her arms and moved to lean on the wall next to her sister.

"For what?" Anne asked, putting her head on Amity's shoulder.

Amity breathed in that familiar scent of laundry detergent and Stella McCartney perfume. "I'm sorry I spent the last of my money on that stupid Audi when I left New York. I wish I'd come here with buckets of cash to shower you and my...niece... nephew?"

"Nice try," Anne said, nudging Amity. "I'm not telling."

Amity sighed. "You never play fair."

"As the younger sister, I don't have many opportunities to be a step ahead of you. I'm seizing this one." Anne laughed. Then she flinched.

Amity sucked in a breath. "You sure that's false labor?"

"Yup," Anne said through gritted teeth. "That's what the doctor said two days ago at my last appointment." She stood up and plucked the flashlight out of Amity's hand. "You know that flashlight doesn't work, right?"

"Don't try to change the subject," Amity started, grabbing the flashlight back.

"I'm serious," Anne said, snatching the flashlight once again. "It needs size C batteries, which we don't have here at the shop. I'll have to bring some from home tomorrow."

Amity bit back a swear word. "I'm not sure Hank is going to be able to diagnose the problem without a better light back in that storage closet. And here I made him spend his off hours helping us out and I can't even give him enough light to see by."

"From the way he was looking at you, I don't think you *made* him do anything." Anne winked. "But if you feel bad about it, you should take him out to the Art Walk tonight. Buy him a cider to make it up to him." An impish smile spread across Anne's rosy cheeks.

"Stop trying to set me up." Amity squinted at her sister.

"I'm not. I think you both deserve a night out. The Christmas Art Walk event is amazing here, and it only happens the two nights before Christmas Eve. You both deserve some fun tonight. You, for agreeing to represent our humble shop at the craft fair this week," Anne mock bowed at her, "and Hank, for trying to help us solve the wifi mystery."

"Mystery solved," Hank's booming bass carried from the direction of the office. He rounded a bookshelf and came into view—a little dustier than when Amity left him. "I think I know what's going on."

"Without a flashlight?" Amity said, waving the pink flashlight at him. "I'm sorry I was taking so long." She poked Anne's shoulder. "Sister trouble."

Anne smirked at her and poked Amity's shoulder in return.

"I used the light on my phone," Hank said. He didn't stop walking when he got to the front counter, but slid around to the right where an antique lamp was plugged in. Bending down, he gave the plug a little jiggle. The lamplight fluttered. "Yup. Pretty sure I know what's going on."

Amity stared at him as he stood. Anne wasn't wrong. He was handsome. He was tall, but not obnoxiously so, with brown hair cut shorter at the sides and left a little longer on top. Not quite a classic Colorado mountain man, but more rugged than an IT guy ought to be.

A slight smile appeared under Hank's five o'clock shadow, and Amity knew instantly that he'd caught her staring. She returned his knowing smile with a pinched smile of her own.

"What's the diagnosis, doc?" Anne asked, hoisting herself off the wall where she'd been leaning.

"It's your electrical," he answered. The lamp flickered again, as if on cue.

"Ha!" Anne barked as Amity groaned. "I was right! I knew it!" Anne pointed her index finger at Amity's face, and Amity playfully batted her sister's hand away.

"Fine. Great," Amity said, pressing two fingers to the space between her eyes. "Is it fixable?"

"Yes," Hank said, leaning on the counter next to the lamp. "But it's not going to be easy. Or cheap. The building has old wiring. It probably should have been updated decades ago. I can check with my sister—she's an architect, and does remodeling now. She'll know how to find out just how out of date it is. It might give you a leg to stand on to ask the building owner to update it."

It was Anne's turn to groan. "Arthur Donnelly would sooner abandon this building than put any money into it."

Hank frowned. "I'm sorry." He put his hands in his pockets. "You can always lodge a complaint with the city…"

Anne cut him off. "The council is in his back pocket." She ran her hands over her curly brown hair, closed her eyes, and took a deep breath. "I need some time to think about my next move. You two should go. Enjoy the Art Walk. Get some cider."

"I'm not going to leave…" Amity began, her eyes flicking to Anne's baby bump.

Anne stopped her. "I'm *fine*. And look, Clyde's back." She pointed her chin at the ebony skinned septuagenarian walking through the front door. "Go. I'm going to head back to the office and put my feet up."

Hank and Amity both glanced at Clyde, who had begun straightening ornaments on the small Christmas tree in the front window, then looked at each other.

"Go," Anne said, pointing at the door. "Shoo."

Amity shrugged. "Buy you a cider?"

"Sounds like heaven," Hank said with a warm smile.

AMITY HAD TO ADMIT, THE LITTLE ROCKY MOUNTAIN TOWN OF ST. Francis outdid itself during the holidays. The retail stretch of Main Street may have only run five blocks long, but every inch of it was a spectacle. Garlands of silver tinsel were strung overhead, giving the ambiance of winter snow without the cold and wet that go along with the real stuff. Electric candles flickered in shop windows, and tastefully decorated Christmas trees stood next to doorways.

Amity took a deep breath. "I love that smell," she whispered.

"Fir trees?" Hank asked, sipping his hot apple cider as they walked.

"Yep." Amity stopped at a blue-themed Christmas tree outside a modern art gallery. Emerald blue blown-glass ornaments dotted the tree between electric blue glass icicles. A light dusting of powder-blue tinsel rounded out the tree's holiday decor. She leaned over, pushed her gray cashmere scarf away from her face, and breathed in the scent. "There's nothing like that smell."

Hank laughed, a rolling sound that moved through Amity's bones and made her shiver.

Amity tilted her head up at him, smiled, and shrugged. "I'm a sucker for the smell of Christmas. Maybe because it's the only time of year in New York I don't just smell car exhaust, body odor, and desperation. Christmas trees literally bring a breath of fresh air to the city."

"You make New York sound wonderful," Hank said with a snort. He stopped at a trash can and put his empty cup in, then reached out his hand to take Amity's. She handed him her empty cup and nodded her thanks.

"Manhattan *is* wonderful. At least, I think so," Amity said. She pulled up her thick scarf and tucked her chin into it. "I grew up there. Until Anne moved here, I had never really spent time anywhere else."

"You didn't travel at all?" Hank walked slowly and Amity kept pace.

"Why would I? You don't have to leave Manhattan to see the world—the world comes to Manhattan."

Hank smiled. "I never thought of it that way." He stopped to stare at the window display of a luggage shop. A stack of rolling luggage in the shape of a tree was crowned with a star made of plane tickets. His smile flipped upside down.

"Not a fan of rolling luggage?" Amity stood next to Hank and elbowed him lightly.

"I don't miss that life," he said, tucking his hands into the pockets of his leather coat.

"I take it you *did* travel."

"I traveled a lot. I was a software installation technician. I'd go into these big corporations and manufacturing companies and install complicated operational software. I lived in Seattle, but I traveled for work more than I was home." Hank looked at his feet, appearing lost in thought.

"Why'd you stop?"

Hank kept his head down, but turned his eyes up at Amity. "All that time on the road took a toll."

Something in Hank's demeanor told Amity not to press. She simply nodded. In the light from the luggage shop window, his eyes looked chocolate brown instead of the stunning forest green she knew they were. His eyes had a depth she hadn't often encountered in her life. Perhaps it was because she had lived so long in the shallows of the Manhattan art scene, but she was intrigued. The stirring in her spirit told her that there was something in those depths worth discovering.

Maybe if she'd taken the time to discover Jonathan, her ex-boyfriend back in New York, she wouldn't be in such trouble now. Amity took a deep breath and tried to stuff down the fear that was rising in her chest.

Hank turned to face her. "Everything okay?"

"Yep," Amity said, crossing her arms. "Let's keep moving. I'm starting to freeze."

Without missing a beat, Hank put his arm around her. His leather coat creaked as his hand wrapped around her upper arm, and her body was enveloped in warmth.

Amity stood as still as a statue. She could suddenly hear the pulse of her own heart, and the flush that normally spread to her cheeks instead ran to her lips. Hank was so close, she could smell the woodsy scent of his aftershave. She locked eyes with him, and she was lost in the forest of green. She leaned into the feeling, and into his embrace. Her lips brushed his for a sweet, brief moment before reality came crashing in.

"I'm leaving town," Amity blurted as she suddenly pulled back. She hadn't planned it, and it came out not just rushed, but brusque.

Hank pulled his arm back. "I see," he said, putting his hands in his pockets.

He looked down, and Amity couldn't gauge his expression. The sudden silence between them was painful—and her compulsion to fill it was overwhelming. "I—I've got an opportunity. In L.A."

Hank tilted his head up and to the side. "Does Anne know?"

Amity shook her head. "She knows about the offer. She doesn't know I'm going to take it."

"When do you leave?"

"Saturday."

"Christmas Eve?"

"I've been invited to attend a party."

"In L.A."

"Yeah."

"On Christmas Eve."

"Yes."

Hank shrugged. "Sounds fancy. If I know sisters, though—and

I do, because I have three of them—you're going to want to steel yourself for a fight."

"Anne knows I wasn't planning on staying forever." Amity frowned.

Hank frowned back. He breathed deeply and inhaled the scent of fresh-cut pine. "Pregnant sister. Christmas Eve. It's ugly math."

"She's going to have to understand," Amity said breathlessly. "This is how I get back on top."

"On top of what?"

"Of my career!"

"Making jewelry?"

"Making art." The heat rising to Amity's cheeks now wasn't a blush, it was the steam of anger. "The jewelry that I make isn't the plastic stuff you find in shops like that," she waved her hand toward a souvenir shop across the street. "It's art. It makes a statement." Amity saw Hank's frown deepen and her anger rose. "You wouldn't understand. You can be a tech guy anywhere."

"And you can't make fancy jewelry anywhere but L.A." Hank phrased it as a statement, not a question, and it was the last straw.

"My designs aren't meant for ski tourists and mountain men," Amity waved a dismissive hand in Hank's direction. "They're meant for collectors. For people who know art."

"And us backward mountain bums wouldn't know art if it bit us on the rear. Gotcha." Hank's nostrils flared.

"You make me sound like a monster for wanting to get my life back." Amity fought down the angry tears threatening to ruin her mascara.

"I just don't see what's wrong with life in a town like St. Francis."

"And I don't see why it's a crime to want more than this dumb little town."

Hank and Amity stood face to face on the sidewalk outside the Bugling Elk coffee shop, fury practically sparking the air between their locked eyes. The petite barista inside put her cleaning rag down and stared at them through the window. Amity noticed her out of the corner of her eye, and broke eye contact with Hank.

"This was a royally bad idea." Amity spun on her heel. "Thanks for helping Anne today. Have a nice life," she said over her shoulder.

She didn't look back to see if Hank was watching her go.

HANK

HANK STOOD, DUMBFOUNDED, IN FRONT OF THE BUGLING ELK AND watched Amity walk away. What just happened? One minute we were having a lovely evening, enjoying the holiday Art Walk, and the next she's telling me this town isn't good enough for her. He shook his head. When he looked up, the barista was looking at him through the window with pity all over her face.

Hank put on a fake smile, nodded at the barista, and walked the opposite direction from where Amity stormed off. He looked at the tidy street decorations and the glowing shop windows. He breathed in the frigid mountain air. And he remembered a time when a life like this seemed so out of reach.

This little town—even with all its problems—was heaven to him. The pace of life was slow. Families looked out for one another here. This was the kind of place where life could finally catch up to you.

The things he'd said to Amity were already eating at him. He knew he had reacted too strongly. But something about Amity's reaction bothered him. He got to the end of the retail stretch of Main Street and turned back around. Walking helped him think. He wasn't ready to go home yet anyway.

Memories of his sisters as teenagers came flooding into his mind. Arguments over hair accessories that got ridiculously out of control...sniping at each other about whose boyfriend was the best...and tears over someone not listening. Hank was the second youngest of the bunch, with one younger sister and two older, but they were all within eighteen to twenty-four months apart in age. The older they got, the closer they all became.

Amity storming off reminded him of a fight between his sisters when he was sixteen years old. His eighteen-year-old sister, Junie, had just been dumped. His nineteen-year-old sister, Rebecca, was home from college, and tried to coax Junie into telling her what happened. Junie didn't want to talk about it, and flew into a rage at Rebecca.

The sisters didn't talk for a month after that.

Now, standing in the Colorado winter cold on a beautiful night, all alone, Hank remembered what Junie explained to him about that fight years later. "I was all feelings," Junie had said. "I couldn't put it into words—I just hurt. Rebecca was trying to make me talk about something I didn't have the words to communicate. I was in pain, and I lashed out."

Had something hurt Amity? And if so, why did that bother him so much?

AMITY

With the walk back to the bookstore to get her car, and the drive up the mountain, it was nine o'clock at night before Amity walked in the door of Anne's house. She slammed the heavy wood door, rattling the windows of the old Victorian and shaking the ornaments on the Christmas tree in the living room.

"Amity?" Anne called from the direction of the kitchen. The sound of running water accompanied her tired voice.

"Yeah, it's me," Amity shouted back. She hung her coat up on the coat rack near the door and kicked off her boots. She caught movement at the top of the stairs and looked up to see her sister's calico cat, Melody, descending the steep old oak staircase. The cat reached the bottom step and stopped, lifting its pink nose in Amity's direction.

"What?" Amity said to the cranky old cat. "You think I'm a snob, too?" She stuck her tongue out at Melody as she passed by on the way to the kitchen.

Anne was sitting at the kitchen table in a floral robe, taking the tags off new baby clothes. "How'd it go?" she asked without looking up. She held up a tiny onesie with a Colorado flag on it, smiled, and sighed.

Amity pulled out a chair from the small kitchen table, and it made an awful scraping noise on the tile floor. She plopped down in the chair, put her elbows on the table, and buried her face in her hands.

The kitchen was as quiet as the forest when it snowed. Amity didn't hear her sister move, but she suddenly felt Anne's warm hand on her back.

"That bad, huh?" Anne asked, rubbing her hand in a circle on the spot between Amity's shoulder blades.

Amity remembered their mother doing the same thing when she was tired but she wanted her daughters to know she was there and listening. It was strange to think that Anne would soon be a mother, too. Amity removed her hands from her face, and looked up at her very pregnant sister. "I need to tell you something."

Anne frowned and turned her chair so she was facing Amity.

Somehow, Anne's chair didn't scrape the way Amity's always did. Anne just always seemed to have a gentler touch. Ever since they were children, Amity had felt like a bull in a china shop—and her sister was a china doll. It wasn't so much about the way they looked, or the way they moved, but with their approach to the world. Amity came at the world hard and fast. Anne was thoughtful about each step. When Anne had called and told her that she had opened a bookshop in this small Colorado mountain town, Amity had been shocked. Not by the bookshop itself—Anne had always been a bookworm—but by the speed and confidence with which Anne had made the decision to do it.

Amity swallowed hard. *There is no good way to say this. I just need to spit it out.* "I've been thinking about the offer to sell my work in L.A."

"Okay..." Anne said, pausing the back rub.

"I'm going to take them up on it. And I have to leave on Saturday."

The silence in the kitchen seemed to echo off the walls. "But that's Christmas Eve," Anne whispered.

"The woman who is spearheading this whole thing wants me at her Christmas Eve party."

"And that's only two days away." Anne's eyes welled.

Amity nodded. "This only just came about yesterday. I'm supposed to get a call tomorrow and confirm I'm coming…"

"So you haven't said yes yet," Anne interrupted.

"Not formally, no. But Anne, I've already decided. I need to do this."

"Why? Why can't you sell your work here?"

Amity rolled her eyes. "You sound just like Hank." She sat back in her chair and crossed her arms.

"Don't you like it here?" Anne had managed to hold back her tears, but she still sounded like a wounded child. "And if Hank is telling you the same thing, that this is a good place to live, shouldn't you just maybe *consider* staying?"

"St. Francis is a sweet little town," Amity said with a sigh. "And it's near enough to Aspen, it's not totally backwoods—it's a great place for you. But I need the art scene. I need to be in community with other serious artists."

"Like the serious artist who drained your business dry and ran off with your assistant to Paris?" It was Anne's turn to sit back and cross her arms.

Amity sucked air through her teeth. "That's a low blow."

"And where were those serious artists when your world collapsed? It seems to me that the art community you ran away from doesn't need you the way you need it. Or maybe they just need your money."

Amity stood so fast, her chair toppled over. "I wouldn't expect you, little Miss Susie Homemaker, to understand. But I would expect you to be more supportive of my career." Her ears felt hot with anger.

"There's more to life than your career, Amity," Anne said quietly.

"Like what?" Amity unclenched her fists and took a deep breath.

"Like family. Like making a home. Like doing what you do for the love of it and not just for the prestige."

"It didn't feel prestigious having to sublet my apartment and move in with my sister halfway across the country." Amity blew out an angry breath. "I don't design jewelry for the prestige. I do it because I love it. And I happen to be good at it. And it pays the bills. I'm just a leech here."

"You're not a leech. You're my sister, and I love you." Anne stood slowly, clutching her belly and wincing as she rose.

Amity rushed to her side. "Are you okay? Sit back down."

"I'm fine. Just Braxton Hicks contractions again."

Amity put her arm around Anne's shoulder and pulled her sister close. Anne leaned on Amity's shoulder, and Amity kissed the top of her head. "I love you. I'm happy you found a home here, and you're making a family here. But I can't stay." Amity felt Anne nod, and let the conversation end there.

"I need to get off my feet. I'm heading to bed," Anne said, pulling away. She didn't look back at Amity until she was halfway down the hall. "I'll miss you," she whispered over her shoulder.

Amity picked up the fallen kitchen chair, then collapsed in it. She kept her sobs quiet so she wouldn't keep her sister awake.

HANK

AS HANK GOT OUT OF HIS TRUCK IN FRONT OF THE CITY government building Friday morning, his cell phone rang shrilly in his pocket. He slammed the door hard to make sure it stayed closed —the last thing he needed was to come back out to snow on his seat and a dead battery again—then fished the phone out of his pocket.

"It's Anne," the bookshop owner greeted him sweetly. "I'm so sorry to bother you, but I need your help again. I'm getting an 'invalid password' error when I try to log in to the wifi network today."

"You should really call your internet provider," Hank said, tilting the phone down a little so he wasn't breathing into the microphone as he walked to the building.

"I've been on hold with them for two hours already," she said. "I can't take any more time away from the front—it's a busy day at the shop. Please? You said you have sisters, right? I'll send signed copies of *Eat, Pray, Love* to each of them if you'll come rescue me!"

Hank laughed. "They do love Elizabeth Gilbert. How did you know?"

"Everyone loves Elizabeth Gilbert. She's an institution," Anne said. "Pretty please?"

Hank's sigh was halfhearted. Anne reminded him so much of his younger sister, Cordelia. He couldn't say no if he wanted to. She had a way of getting past his strongest defenses.

"Okay. Fine," Hank said as he walked in the sliding door at the front of the city building. "But you've got to send them each one of Amity's fancy bookmarks, too." His heart clenched a little when he said her name.

"Deal," Anne said. "When can you get here?"

"I'll come over during my lunch hour. Be there at noon."

"You're a lifesaver."

"Don't praise me yet. I don't know if I can fix your problem." Hank walked up the linoleum steps toward his office on the second floor.

"I know you can," Anne said.

THE SCENT OF CINNAMON AND CLOVES WASHED OVER HANK WHEN he walked into Booktopia one minute past noon. He closed his eyes and breathed deep. Between the notes of holiday spices, he smelled the leathery scent of unopened books and the musty scent of well-loved ones.

The table display right in front of the door was different than it was yesterday. Yesterday it was covered in novels with holiday themes. Today it was covered in children's books. Hank stepped up and picked up a colorfully illustrated copy of *'Twas the Night Before Christmas*.

"Mary Engelbreit," said the smiling, stooped old man walking Hank's direction. "She's one of my favorite illustrators. You like her work?"

"I've never heard of her," Hank responded. "But I have a niece who would love this." He turned the large yet slim book over in his hands.

"That's why we put these beauties out right before Christmas. It's the perfect time to buy frivolous and beautiful books for the children in your life." The bookseller's white teeth gleamed against his dark skin when he smiled.

Hank held the book out toward the man, and noted the name "Clyde" printed neatly on the nametag pinned to his red flannel shirt. "Can you keep this at the counter for me? I'm actually here to help the owner fix the wifi."

"Ah! I remember you. You came in yesterday, and I was too distracted to do much more than point you to the back office. Hank, right?" The man took the book in one hand and extended the other. "I'm Clyde."

Hank took Clyde's proffered hand and shook it gently. The man looked brittle—but he had a surprisingly strong grip. "Nice to meet you," Hank said.

"Anne is in the back office. You know the way?" Clyde tilted his head toward the back of the shop.

Hank nodded and took a step toward the odd yet cozy office at the back of the bookshop.

"I'll keep this up front for you," Clyde said, waving the book in Hank's direction.

"Thanks. I may do a little more shopping before I leave, too. If I get a book for one niece, I need to get one for all of them." Hank laughed.

"You're not wrong," Clyde said with a wink.

Hank wound his way through the shelves of neatly organized books, pens, notecards, and other reading and writing accoutrements. When he reached the office door, he noticed it was cracked, and he heard voices coming from inside.

When he pushed the door open, he found Anne and Amity facing off.

Amity turned her big, dark eyes at him, and he melted a little in the split second before she rolled those eyes at him. "Great," she said.

"You two need to sort this out," Anne said, glaring at her sister, her arms crossed over her pregnant belly. Her chocolate brown hair was tied back in a messy bun fit for a librarian.

"Why?" Hank said sharply. "She'll be gone tomorrow anyway."

Anne's typically serene expression contorted and she collapsed into sobs.

Amity seemed shocked by the abrupt change in her sister, and she threw her arms around Anne. "It's okay," she whispered. "Please don't cry." Fury blazed in Amity's eyes as she looked at Hank over Anne's shoulder.

Hank stepped further into the room. "I'm sorry, Anne. I didn't mean to make you cry." He put his hand on Amity's shoulder, her black hair brushing his knuckles gently. "Let's get her to a chair," he said softly.

Amity nodded, then gently guided her sister to one of the club chairs in front of the fireplace.

Anne sniffed and wiped her nose with the back of her hand as she carefully lowered her swollen body into the chair. "You two need to get along. Even if it's just for one more day," she said. "Amity, I need Hank's help. And Hank, you need Amity to make more of those bookmarks you want for your sisters, because we're sold out."

"I don't need the bookmarks…" Hank started.

Anne made a *tsk*ing noise at him and waved her finger. "No. You need them."

Hank and Amity looked at each other, and Hank recognized the helpless look on her face. He made that same face every time one of his nieces asked him for a favor.

Anne put her hand on her belly and groaned. "I'm starving. Will you two please go get me some food? I'm craving paneer masala from India Palace."

Amity closed her eyes, shook her head, and smiled. "Anne…"

"Please?" Anne said, her brown eyes pleading.

"I only have an hour before I need to head back to work," Hank said, glancing at his watch.

"I'll call ahead," Anne said. "It'll be ready when you get there. Please?" Her pout deepened.

Amity smiled indulgently at her sister, and for the first time Hank noticed that one of her lateral incisors stuck out further than the rest of her teeth. He resisted the urge to chuckle out loud. It was a delight to see a little flaw in her perfect veneer.

Hank met Amity's eyes. They were less angry than last night, but no less complicated. He raised his eyebrows in her direction.

Amity shrugged. "Fine. But you're driving."

AMITY

AMITY BUCKLED THE LAP BELT IN THE PASSENGER SEAT OF THE OLD blue pickup. The interior smelled like chopped wood and the ancient remnants of cigarette smoke.

"Your sister is incorrigible," Hank said as he slid in behind the steering wheel. He slammed the door so hard, the entire truck rocked.

Amity couldn't stop the smile from crossing her lips, though she didn't want to be friendly with this frustrating man. "I was helpless to resist her before she was pregnant. Now...I'm practically her slave."

"I can see why," Hank said. He started the engine and it roared to life with the sound akin to mountain thunder.

"Did you used to smoke?" Amity asked, sniffing the air.

"Hmm?" Hank kept his eyes on the road as he pulled out of the parking space and onto Main Street.

"It smells a little like smoke in here. But *you* don't smell like smoke."

"And what do I smell like?" Hank asked with a coy smile.

Heat rose to Amity's cheeks and she turned her head to look out the passenger side window.

"This truck was my grandfather's," Hank said after a moment of awkward silence. "He smoked heavily. When he passed on nine years ago, I inherited this old blue beast. It sat in storage for seven years. Couldn't believe it started up right away when I was getting ready to move here. My ex took my brand new Chevy pickup in the divorce. I wasn't sure this ancient Ford was going to make the trip to Colorado, but here we are two years later and it's still running strong."

Amity was surprised at the tightness in her chest. "You were married before?"

"Yup. We lasted three years." Hank turned onto Yucca Rd and the restaurant came into view.

"What happened?" Amity felt compelled to ask...but she wasn't entirely sure she wanted the answer.

"I traveled for my job. She got lonely."

"Why didn't you change jobs?"

"I loved my job." Hank pulled into a parking spot in front of India Palace and turned off the engine. He frowned at his hands on the steering wheel. "I loved her, though, too. She didn't tell me she was that lonely until it was too late. Someone else was giving her the attention she needed. To be honest...I think I knew she needed me home. I think I was just scared that I would resent her if I quit my job for her." He chuckled dryly. "Funny. I resented her a lot more when she left me for her dentist."

"Ouch," Amity said, putting her hand over her heart.

They looked at each other across the cab of the truck, only Amity's small silver purse separating them on the wide bench seat. Amity broke eye contact first. She grabbed her purse, then opened the door and stepped out into the cold mountain air.

When Amity closed the truck door, she could tell it hadn't latched properly. Before she could open and close it again, Hank was next to her. He put his hand over hers on the door handle. He still smelled like sandalwood and fir.

"You've got to give it a good shove," he said softly

He was so close to her, she could feel the heat of his breath on her ear. A shiver ran up her spine. She pulled her hand back and stepped to the side so he could close the truck door properly.

Hank took the lead as they walked up to the restaurant together. He opened the door and held it for Amity. She nodded politely and walked into the dimly lit interior of India Palace.

"Can I help you?" a voice said from behind the register.

Amity jumped a little and clutched her stomach, not realizing the young woman was there until she spoke. "Oh! Hi. Yes, I'm picking up an order for Anne Parish."

"Just this?" the woman asked as she handed a small bag over the counter. Her wrists gleamed with gold bangles, highlighting her bronze skin. "Nothing for you?" Her deep brown eyes squinted with amusement.

"I could use a bite…" Hank said.

Amity looked over her shoulder at him and shrugged. "I'm hungry too. But I don't want to make Anne wait."

The young woman cleared her throat. "We have a buffet. You can take food to go." She pointed toward the back of the restaurant.

"Sold," Hank said with a smile.

Amity liked that smile. Even if she didn't particularly like the man.

Before long, Hank and Amity were back in the truck with enough food to feed a small army. The truck cab no longer smelled like smoke, but instead smelled of curry and naan bread. Amity's stomach growled loudly. Hank laughed, that deep, warm sound that gave Amity a fluttery feeling inside.

"I'm glad you didn't say no to getting food," Hank said as he started the engine. "Your stomach is louder than my truck."

Silence filled the space between them until Hank turned the truck back onto Main Street.

"What about…" Hank started.

"Thanks for…" Amity spoke at the same moment Hank did.

They both laughed awkwardly.

"You first," Amity said with a smile.

Hank shook his head. "I was just going to ask…" he paused a beat. "Were you ever married?"

"No." Amity was quick to answer. "I had a serious boyfriend back in New York. I thought we'd eventually get married. But… that didn't happen."

"Why did you break up?"

Amity took a deep breath and turned to look out the side window. When she looked back at Hank, she noticed a furrow between his brows. Something inside her ached to relieve whatever worry was causing that sweet wrinkle over his green eyes.

"He embezzled from my jewelry business. Then he stole what remained, and ran off to Paris with my assistant."

"I was not expecting that," Hank said. He parked the truck in front of the bookshop.

"Neither was I," Amity said, laughing in spite of herself. Then she found she couldn't *stop* laughing. "It's so ridiculous. I mean, I'm embarrassed that I didn't see right through him. And the man ruined me. But telling the story…it's like the plot to a terrible novel: Man runs off with assistant and leaves woman nearly bankrupt, and she must start over against all odds."

Amity's phone rang shrilly in her purse. She pulled it out and her heart sped up a little when she saw a California area code before the phone number on the screen. *It's now or never.* She looked at Hank out of the corner of her eye. "I need to take this," she said, waving the phone. She hopped out of the truck, put her box of takeout on the hood, and took a few steps down the sidewalk away from Hank before she answered the call.

"Amity Green here," she said pleasantly into the receiver.

"Amity, it's Carl. From L.A."

"Carl, it's great to hear from you."

"I'll cut to the chase. I'm leaving tomorrow. My wife wants you as her special guest at her Christmas Eve party, and we've got a glass case with your name on it in our showroom on Rodeo. You in?"

Amity opened her mouth to answer and saw her sister emerge from the bookshop. Anne was clutching her lower back with one hand, and taking a bag of food from Hank with the other. They say pregnant women have a glow about them—but Anne simply radiated. Hank smiled warmly at her and motioned for her to go back inside. He followed her into Booktopia, and Amity was suddenly alone on the sidewalk. The cold mountain breeze tickled her cheek. The scent of cinnamon and old books wafted from the shop entryway.

"Amity, you there?" Carl's voice boomed in her ear.

Amity jumped. "Sorry," she said, brushing her bangs off her forehead with her index finger. "I'm here."

"Are you flying out with me tomorrow? My assistant needs to let our pilot know right away so he can update the itinerary."

"Private plane?"

"Of course. You didn't think I flew commercial from L.A. to Aspen, did you?" Carl laughed gruffly.

Visions of fancy parties, fancier dresses, and cocktail-fueled conversations about the meaning of modern art danced in front of Amity's eyes. She forced herself not to look back at Booktopia or Hank's truck, though the pull was strong.

"I'm coming," she said into the phone. Her voice broke a little, but her resolve didn't.

HANK

HANK STOOD AT THE COUNTER TALKING TO CLYDE AND ANNE, WHO was behind the register scarfing down paneer masala like her life depended on it, when the bell over the door jingled. They all turned to see a heavyset man in a cheap suit trudge in.

"That's Arthur Donnelly," Anne whispered over a mouthful of food. She elbowed Hank.

Hank was surprised to see that Arthur looked nothing like his daughter, Tricia. Where Tricia was slim and blonde, Arthur was round and balding. But entitlement and overconfidence clearly ran in the family.

"What's this I hear about you asking for my building mainte-nance records?" Arthur's raspy voice carried across the blessedly empty bookshop.

Anne swallowed her food as the blood drained from her face. "I didn't..."

"I did," Hank said quickly, noticing her discomfort.

"Who the hell are you?" Arthur demanded, nearly out of breath by the time he reached the three of them at the register. His tone may have been menacing, but his red cheeks made him look like a comic book gangster.

"Hank Drummond. I work for the city." It was the truth, if not the whole truth. Hank pulled himself up to his full height as Arthur approached.

The round little man waved a finger in Hank's direction. "Why are you nosing into my business?"

"Because the electrical system in this building is ancient, and it's directly affecting the livelihood of one of St. Francis's finest retailers."

"Finest retailers. Ha! She sells musty old books." Arthur pulled a handkerchief out of the breast pocket of his blue checkered sport coat and coughed violently into it. "See? I cough every time I walk in here. It's *musty*."

"I'll have you know I sell new and used books," Anne said, crossing her arms over her belly. "And none of our products are *musty*. This building is musty. Or should I say moldy."

"I've had mold inspectors out here twice, thanks to your bogus complaints," Arthur railed at her.

"And how much did you pay the inspectors to ignore the big black stains in the bathroom ceiling?" Clyde jumped in. Anne nodded at him.

"Everything is above board," Arthur rattled. He slid his watery brown eyes toward Hank. "Including the electrical system."

"The building loses power when you plug in a lamp," Hank said. "There's no way this building is up to code."

"This building is a historic landmark," Arthur countered. "My responsibility is to maintain the integrity of the property, and updating the electrical system would alter the building. The only updates I have to do involve finding new tenants." He squinted at Anne. "Your lease is up in less than a year. Stop causing trouble or find yourself a new location to sell your musty books." With that, he turned on his heel and strode toward the front door—nearly bowling Amity over on the way.

A look of concern was etched on Amity's alabaster face as she approached the register. "What is that old curmudgeon doing here?" She said in a low voice, throwing a glance over her shoulder when the bell over the door alerted them that Arthur had exited the store.

"I had my sister request the maintenance records on this building," Hank said. "I didn't think for a second that Arthur would find out, much less link it back to Anne."

"The man's got eyes everywhere," Anne said through a bite of Indian food. "I would have warned you if I thought you were serious about having your sister pull the records."

"Why wouldn't I be serious?" Hank asked.

"People say they'll help, but then they don't," Anne said with a shrug.

"When I say I'm going to do something," Hank said, his eyes squaring, "I do it." He looked to his right to see Amity staring at him like he'd grown a third eye. "What?" he asked her.

Amity shook her head. "Nothing. It's just…it's really sweet of you to get involved. You don't know us. But here you are fixing Booktopia's wifi and helping us expose Arthur Donnelly's scam."

"Whoa," Hank said. "I didn't say anything about exposing anyone."

"So you think the man is honest?" Amity asked.

Hank looked from side to side. Anne and Clyde were behind the counter, looking like they were holding their breath. Amity was shooting daggers at him with her dark eyes.

"Oh no," he said. "The man is a total sleaze. Trying to slither out of his responsibilities as a landlord by having this building designated as a historic landmark? That's a sleaze move." Hank didn't need any of these people to like him. He wasn't saying this to impress them. Arthur was just like every slumlord his dad had had to deal with as a tenants' attorney in Seattle. Hank hadn't met many of them in person—but he'd heard enough stories to be able to spot a sleaze-bag a mile away.

Amity had stopped glaring at him now. Her eyes were soft

with what he imagined was relief. She put her hand on his arm. "Can you help us?"

"Us?" Anne said to Amity, her voice tentative.

Hank saw an unspoken conversation happening between the two sisters.

The silence went on too long and Hank was beginning to feel awkward. "Rebecca, my sister, must have gotten the records. I don't know why she hasn't called me about it, but I'll follow up with her and let you know what we figure out." He looked at his watch. "Damn. I have to get back to the office. I'm sorry I didn't get to fix your wifi."

Anne shrugged. "I was able to get logged in while you guys got the food. It's a Christmas miracle."

Amity put her hand over her eyes and shook her head. Clyde guffawed.

"Christmas miracle, huh?" Hank lifted an eyebrow in Anne's direction, but she wouldn't meet his gaze. He sighed. "I'll let you know what I find out about the building records. Meanwhile, don't get into online gaming. Or plug too many things into one outlet. Or really just use too much bandwidth or electricity in general."

Anne and Amity nodded at him. Clyde grunted a thank-you. And with that, Hank walked back out into the Colorado sunshine.

WHEN HANK EMERGED FROM THE DIM BOOKSHOP INTO THE BRIGHT daylight, Arthur Donnelly was sitting in his Mercedes three spaces down from Hank's truck. The two men stared at each other as Hank circled the front end of his old pickup and climbed into the driver's side.

Hank placed both hands on the steering wheel and took a calming breath. Just when he thought his heart had regained its natural rhythm, it sped up again at the sound of the passenger door opening.

Amity slid onto the bench seat and pulled the door shut firmly.

"Hello," Hank said, his hands still on the steering wheel.

"Hi." Amity sat primly, facing the front windshield, with only her head turned toward Hank.

In the silence of the cab, Hank finally had a moment to take her in. Amity wore a black pencil skirt over gray knit tights, and her hands were perched lightly on her thighs. Her nails were pristine, with no polish that he could see—though maybe it was one of those French manicures his sisters talked about. The collar was turned up on her puffy black coat, and her hair was tucked neatly into it, drawing attention to her big, dark eyes. Hank could feel himself drowning in them.

"Thank you," Amity said curtly.

"For what?"

"For helping my sister. You didn't have to."

"Men like Donnelly need to be reminded that the law applies to them just as much as it does to the rest of us."

Amity nodded. "Still. I worry about Anne. It makes me feel better to know there are people looking out for her here."

"Because you're leaving."

"Because she's a good person, and she deserves to be looked out for."

Hank frowned. "How is she handling you moving to L.A.?"

"Not well," Amity said with a shake of her head.

Hank reached out and plucked her left hand off her leg. He gently squeezed her delicate fingers, and found himself lingering there, holding her hand. The temperature rose in the cab of the truck. As Hank's pulse sped up, he noticed fog was forming on the passenger side window next to Amity. He pulled her hand toward him, and she followed his lead, sliding toward him on the worn bench seat.

"She'll be okay," Hank said in a near whisper. "Donnelly's on my radar now. I'll keep an eye."

Amity's tender smile lifted her face and lit the flame in her eyes. "Thank you," she breathed, putting her free hand on his cheek. As suddenly as she had entered his truck, she put her lips on his. Her mouth was soft and sweet, but her kiss was electric.

Hank wrapped his hands around her back and pulled her tight. Amity turned her body so it was up against his, hiked up her skirt, and slid her leg between his. Hank cursed the steering wheel for preventing her from fully straddling him. Every inch of his body throbbed, and he ached to thrust his hips into her leg.

Their kiss deepened as Amity probed lightly with her tongue. She ran her hand across his shoulder and down his arm, motioning for him to pull her in tighter. He obliged. Her body was soft yet firm in his hands as she moved her mouth from his lips to his neck.

Hanks eyes were half closed, but it was enough to see movement in front of his truck. With a sudden intake of breath, he grabbed Amity by the shoulders and gently but firmly moved her off of him—regretting it instantly. Replacing his view of her flushed cheeks and black hair, now Arthur Donnelly stood facing him.

Amity gasped when she finally noticed why Hank had moved her aside. Donnelly placed one fat hand on the front of Hank's truck, and squinted his colorless eyes at them both.

AMITY

"AND THEN HE GOT OUT OF THE TRUCK AND YELLED, 'HANDS OFF, Donnelly!' I couldn't believe it. The whole thing was surreal." Amity still felt flushed, several hours after the incident in front of the bookshop. As she regaled her sister across the kitchen table, she couldn't get Hank's furious expression out of her mind.

"Were you scared?" Anne asked, putting her hand on Amity's. "You should have called the cops."

Amity shook her head. "No, it was over too quick. The men squared off, then Donnelly walked back to his car and drove away. Besides, we know Donnelly has the local government in his back pocket. And the shop belongs to him…"

"No, the *building* belongs to him. The shop belongs to me and Mark," Anne corrected. "I can't remember the last time I saw you this worked up." Anne squeezed Amity's hand. "Can I make you some tea?"

Amity looked at her sister's swollen belly, perched over swollen feet, and shook her head. "I'm okay. I just…The passion in Hank's eyes. I don't think I've ever seen anything like that. The only thing Jonathan ever got even remotely passionate about was money. We used to have the best sex after I sold a big piece."

"Did you ever stop and wonder?" Anne asked softly. "I mean, did he ever give you an indication that he would steal from you?"

Amity swallowed, then took a deep breath. "I think I knew. Maybe I was just in denial. After Mom died, and you moved here, I made my own family in New York. I didn't want to see Jonathan for who he really was, because he was all I had."

Anne frowned and leaned back in her chair.

"I'm not angry that you left," Amity said quickly. "Or upset. Please know that. This was a good decision for you and Mark. You have a good life here—even with the Donnelly drama. New York was all I knew, and even though the art scene was cutthroat, Jonathan made it comfortable for me. He doted on me when I was successful, and that made me want success even more. I think, underneath it all, I knew it wasn't me he wanted. It was my reputation, and then eventually my money." Tears welled in Amity's eyes, and it surprised her how raw it all still felt. She swallowed again and bid the tears to stop so she could keep talking. "If he had just run off with my money, I wouldn't have been so shocked. It would have been devastating, but it would have made some sense, I think. When he ran off with my money *and ran off to Paris with Lia*, though...I didn't see that coming."

As she spoke, visions of Hank's face danced in her mind, a stark contrast to the narrow, calculating face of her ex-partner. She thought of Hank's firm hands and his soft kisses, and her whole body shivered.

"You cold?" Anne asked, leaning over and rubbing her hand up and down Amity's arm.

"I'm fine," Amity answered. "But I need to change the subject." She stood up from the table and looked at her sister fondly. "I have a little something for you."

"Christmas isn't until Sunday," Anne said with a frown.

Amity looked at her feet and said quietly, "I know. But I want to give it to you before I leave, and I don't want this to feel like a parting gift."

Anne opened her mouth to say something, but Amity didn't give her the chance. She left the kitchen and walked upstairs to the small guestroom she'd been staying in. There was just enough room for a queen-size bed, one scuffed oak nightstand, and a tall oak dresser. She opened the top dresser drawer and pulled out a flat gray box tied with a green ribbon.

Amity ran down the stairs so quickly, she nearly tripped over the cat on the bottom step. "Melody, are you trying to kill me?" she yelled at the unmoving calico. The cat lazily tilted its head at Amity and gave a curt meow. Amity stepped wide to avoid crushing the contemptuous old feline, then made her way back to the kitchen.

Anne was still sitting at the kitchen table, her elbows perched, and her forehead in her hands. She didn't move when Amity pulled a chair out and sat next to her.

"Are you alright?" Amity asked, softly stroking Anne's messy curls.

Anne looked up from her hands. Her eyes were rimmed with red, and she was holding her breath. "False labor again," she said with a shrug, but her coffee-colored eyes betrayed the truth.

Amity didn't want to fight with her sister on her last night in St. Francis. "Maybe we should get you to the hospital," Amity said, pulling her hand back.

"They will just send me home. Braxton Hicks contractions are painful, but normal." Anne gasped and grabbed her stomach.

"This doesn't seem normal." Amity put her hand over her sister's hand on her stomach. "I'm worried about you."

"Then don't leave." Anne managed a weak smile.

Amity sat back, crossed her arms, and narrowed her eyes. "Is this a game? Are you acting? I've made my decision…"

"To go get your career back on track, yeah, I know. But you could have a *life* here."

Once again, the feel of Hank's hands on her back echoed through Amity's body. She looked at her sister, who clearly was in pain—though Amity was sure that wasn't why her eyes were red. The kitchen smelled faintly of stew, and small snowflakes fell outside the window over the sink. In the silence between their words, Amity could hear the tick-tick of the grandfather clock in the hallway, inherited from their grandparents many years ago. This was the closest Amity had ever felt to having a home since she was a child.

And it scared her to death.

"I'll visit," Amity said, standing. She pushed the flat box across the table toward her sister. "Merry Christmas."

With that, Amity left the house, got into the Audi parked under the carport out front, and headed down the hill toward town to clear her head.

IN THE MONTH SHE'D LIVED IN ST. FRANCIS, AMITY HAD LEARNED the town's streets well enough to get to most places without a map. Tonight, though, with a fraught mind and a heavy heart, she didn't have it in her to figure out where she was going. She simply made a beeline for the place she knew best.

Amity pulled her car into one of the many empty spaces in front of Booktopia. The snow had stopped, but it had left an earthy yet celestial scent that only a fresh snow could produce. As Amity got out of her car, she stood in the open door and took a deep lungful of that crisp, fragrant air. Grabbing her scarf off the back of the seat, she pushed the car door closed and began to walk down Main Street.

At 8:30 p.m., the half moon, street lamps, and store window displays lit her path. For a Friday night downtown and the night before Christmas Eve, Amity was surprised at how few people were out. She was also relieved. Her heart hurt with a radiating pain—like anyone coming near would feel what she felt. She didn't know where she was going that night, but she knew she needed to walk. It was a habit she kept from her lifetime in New York—when life gets hard, hit the pavement. Walking could unwind knots and soothe fears. It could calm nerves and stir passions. It was a cure-all.

Maybe Anne is right. Maybe I could have a life here. But what kind of life would it be? I'm not the quiet little mountain town type. I suppose Aspen isn't that far. Maybe it wouldn't be all bad here. Ah, what am I thinking? Amity's mind spun in circles. Lost in thought, she suddenly tripped over a crack she hadn't seen in the sidewalk. Amity caught herself against the side of a red brick building, and stayed leaning there for a moment, staring at her feet. When she lifted her head, she saw two familiar faces in the window of the Italian restaurant across the street.

Hank and Tricia appeared to be having a candlelit dinner for two.

Amity all but ran back to her car. *What was I thinking?*

HANK

WHEN HANK GOT HOME THAT NIGHT, IT WAS 10 P.M. AND HE WAS, regrettably, stone cold sober. Dinner with Tricia Bonham would have been much easier to bear with a good buzz—but he knew he'd have to drive home.

When he had run into Tricia that evening at the grocery store, he hadn't thought much of it. When she followed him out to his car, batting her eyelashes and talking about "two powerful forces in St. Francis government," he had laughed it off. He managed servers and networks, and directed Justin and a few other IT support people to fix computers and set up fax machines. Hank was anything but a "powerful force in government." But when Tricia had invited him to dinner to talk about how they might work together to make the city a better place, it had struck Hank as an opportunity.

The dinner itself was fine. Vicini's fettuccine Alfredo never disappointed. The company and conversation, however, were awkward. Hank had had to walk the line between not leading Tricia on, but still getting all the information he needed about how the city runs its historic preservation program.

Now, safe at home, he felt relieved that he made it through

dinner unscathed. He opened the medicine cabinet in the small master bathroom and rummaged around for a bottle of antacid. *That woman could give heartburn to a block of ice.* Hank laughed at his own joke as his hand found the bottle of chalky chewable tablets.

After changing into clean boxers and an old t-shirt, Hank walked into the living room of his small apartment and plopped down on the pristine charcoal-colored couch. It still had that stiffness in the cushions that only brand-new furniture had. Hank pulled a quilt over his legs (a gift from his youngest sister two Christmases ago that he still loved and used every day), picked up a book from the side table, and flipped to the book-marked page.

As he cracked the book open, his heart caught in his throat at the sight of the delicately beaded crystal bookmark inside. He picked it up and turned it in his hand. It was dainty and exquisite, but at the same time strong and complex. *Just like its designer.* Hank sighed. He put the bookmark back in its place and snapped the book shut.

Grabbing his cell phone off the back of the couch, he dialed Amity's number before he could overthink the decision.

"What?" Amity answered on the second ring.

Her curt voice took Hank by surprise, and it took him a beat to find his words. "Well hello to you too," he said playfully.

"I don't have time for games, Hank. I'm packing."

"You're still planning to go to L.A.?"

"Of course I am."

"I just thought, after yesterday…in the truck…"

"What did you think, exactly?" Amity's voice was ice cold now. "That you could make out with me, then take Tricia out to dinner, and everything would be rosy?"

Hank swallowed. "It's not what you…"

"Oh, don't start. I know exactly how men like you work. I'm

going to make this really easy on you. Pick Tricia. I don't want you." With that, Amity hung up.

Hank stared at the phone screen until it dimmed and then turned black. *That is not how I thought that conversation was going to go*. He touched the phone screen and looked at the time. Then he grabbed the laptop that was sitting on the table next to him. When it booted up, Hank opened a new email and began to write.

"Hey Becks…I've got an idea."

AMITY

CHRISTMAS EVE MORNING, AMITY AWOKE AT DAWN. SHE TOOK ONE last look around the guestroom she'd been living in, making sure one last time that everything was packed into a suitcase or box.

She didn't have much to account for, in the end. She sold most of her belongings before she left New York, and put what remained into a mobile storage unit that she could pay to have transported to wherever she ended up. When she drove her Audi from New York to Colorado a month ago, she'd brought only two suitcases and two boxes with her—mostly full of clothes and jewelry-making supplies. Amity hadn't bought much since she got to St. Francis, but it was enough that the suitcases couldn't hold it all anymore. She hoped that her sister wouldn't give her a hard time about shipping three boxes out to L.A.

As Amity slid out of her bedroom with the two large suitcases in tow, she tried to keep quiet and not wake her sister. From the email Carl's assistant had forwarded her with the flight information, it didn't seem like she'd have to get to the airport nearly as early as she was used to. Apparently, when you own a private jet, you get to bypass little things like checking your bags or going through security. Still, she'd rather get there early…and avoid a dramatic, tearful goodbye with her sister.

"You weren't going to say goodbye?" Anne's weak voice came from behind where Amity stood at the top of the stairs.

"I wrote a letter," Amity said without turning around, afraid that if she met her sister's eyes, she'd change her mind.

"A letter? Damnit, Amity. You're my *sister*. You've been living in my home. You owe me a proper goodbye."

Amity ground her teeth and willed the tears to stay put. She dropped her bags, spun around, and rushed into her sister's arms. "I'm sorry. I'm sorry for all of it. For intruding on your life. For taking up space here in your home. For not wanting to stay. For all of it."

"Sshh," Anne whispered into Amity's hair. "There's nothing to be sorry for."

The sisters hugged each other and cried until Amity finally felt like there were no more tears left to shed. Amity's black turtleneck was soaked, but she didn't care. She squeezed Anne tight.

Anne suddenly gasped, pushed Amity away, and looked at the floor. "I think my water just broke." She looked at Amity with panic in her eyes.

"But you aren't due for weeks!" Amity wailed.

"I don't think the baby cares!"

"What do we do?"

"Get me to the hospital. And call Mark. And get me a towel!" Anne frantically pointed at the linen closet behind Amity.

Amity got Anne down the stairs and settled into a chair in the living room, tucking a stack of towels under her. She took another stack of towels out to the Audi and piled them on the passenger seat. As she ran around, she tried to call her brother-in-law—but Mark wasn't picking up.

"Does Mark turn off his phone when he's sleeping? And what

time does he wake up?" Amity shouted as she ran back into the house.

"No, and usually around 6:30. Why?" Anne said, a hint of panic in her voice.

"He's not picking up."

Anne began to sob.

"I'll get a hold of him. Don't worry. For now, let's get you to the hospital." Amity put her arm around her sister's waist and lifted. "Come on."

With shuffling steps, they made it to the open front door— only to see Hank standing on the other side.

HANK

When Hank had made the decision to go to Anne Parish's house to try to talk to Amity in person that morning before she left for the airport, he had worried about her slamming the door in his face. He had worried about her yelling at him in front of her sister. And he had worried about getting no answer at all when he knocked. What he had *not* worried about was Anne going into labor.

"Move out of the way," Amity snapped at Hank as she helped her sister through the doorway. "Anne needs to get to the hospital."

"I'll drive you. Get in my truck," Hank said, quickly walking back to his old pickup and unlocking the passenger side door.

"I am capable of driving her to the hospital," Amity said, moving toward the Audi.

Hank rolled his eyes. "Don't be stupid." He immediately regretted his choice of words, but there was no time to fix it now. "Anne can lie down on the bench seat if she needs to. And you can call ahead to the hospital more safely if I'm driving. Besides, my truck won't get as messed up as your pretty little sports car."

"I've got towels in the Audi," Amity said.

Hank rushed over, pulled the towels out of Amity's car, and slammed the door closed. Then he put the towels on the passenger seat of his truck.

Amity yelled profanities at him.

"Stop arguing and trust me," Hank demanded. "It got really cold last night, and the hill is slick this morning. This is safer. And I know my way to the hospital. Do you?"

Anne groaned and clutched her belly.

Amity looked at her sister with fear in her eyes. "Fine," she said, and walked Anne over to the truck. The crunch of gravel under their feet echoed in the sudden silence.

"Amity, you sit in the middle and Anne can put her head on you if she needs to lie down." Hank said as he helped the women up into the cab.

"Please get Mark," Anne sobbed as they began the winding drive down the mountain and into town.

"I'll keep trying," Amity said, hitting the dial button. She put it to her ear, and Hank could hear it ringing and ringing. It finally went to a voicemail box with a "this mailbox is full" message.

"He said he only had one planning session left with his team, and he'd head home mid-morning," Anne said between deep breaths and pain-filled groans. "Maybe he's already on his way. Maybe he just doesn't have a signal in the mountains."

"Yeah," Amity said. "I'm sure that's it."

Hank slowed to take a tight turn gently so he wouldn't throw Anne into the door. "Well, there's an upside to all this," he said with a half smile. "Looks like you're getting an early Christmas present."

AMITY

Amity paced the tiny waiting room and chewed her nails. "This is taking too long." She looked at the slim watch on her wrist and tilted it so she could see its ridiculously small face.

Hank sat forward in an ancient, padded chair, elbows on his knees. "I think it takes a while to have a baby. Just based on what I've experienced with my sisters having my nieces and nephew."

"Someone should have come out and told us what's going on. Given us some news. Something. It's 11 a.m. They should have let me back there with her." Amity felt like her heart was going to jump right out of her chest and bounce down the hall to her sister's room.

"Pandemic protocols are still in place here in Colorado. It's for her safety," Hank said.

"I'm family."

"You don't have your vaccine card with you."

"And whose fault is that? I got all...confused when you showed up." Amity's cheeks flared.

Hank chuckled. "Confused, huh?"

"Yes. Confused. I had everything under control until you butted in."

Hank stood and put his hands on his hips. The upper sleeves of his flannel shirt pulled tight against his biceps. "I came to help. I feel like that's all I've been trying to do since I met you, and all *you've* done is give me a hard time."

"I don't need your help," Amity said. Her voice came out weaker than she wanted it to.

The door to the waiting room swung open and a doctor in blue scrubs and a matching face mask walked through. "Amity Green?"

"That's me," Amity said, rushing over to him. Hank stood behind her, and she had to admit that his presence was reassuring.

"I'm Dr. French," the physician said, peering at her with blue eyes over his surgical mask. "Your sister's labor isn't progressing, and we're going to put her on a Pitocin drip to see if we can move things along."

Amity's pulse went into overdrive. "What do you mean, it's not progressing? Her water broke."

Dr. French nodded, and he projected a calm reassurance with his eyes. "Yes, and that's the problem. Once the water breaks, we have 24 hours to deliver the baby. And your sister's not dilating."

Amity stared blankly at the doctor.

Hank cleared his throat. "Correct me if I'm wrong, doc, but that means that Anne's body isn't ready to push the baby out, yet, but the amniotic fluid sustaining the baby's life has drained out. Right?"

"Yes, that's correct. The Pitocin should speed things along. And if it doesn't, we're looking at a C-section."

Amity felt like she was going to faint. She reached back and grabbed Hank's arm to steady herself. Hank put his hand over hers, and she felt the world stop spinning. "We need to get Mark. Anne is going to be freaking out in there." She closed her eyes, took a deep breath, and turned to Hank. "I'm sorry about before. I do need your help."

Hank smiled gently, his green eyes alight. "I know."

"Don't make a thing out of it," Amity grumbled.

Hank chuckled. "I won't." He patted her hand. "You want me to head to Denver, don't you."

Amity nodded. "I'll give you the address where Mark's company planning session was supposed to be taking place. It's Christmas Eve, and everyone should have already gone home, but maybe you'll get lucky and someone there will know how to find him." She frowned, pressing her lips together tightly. "He shouldn't even be there. This thing was supposed to wrap up last night, but he told Anne he needed one more meeting with his team to feel like they really had a handle on this deal. He should have been here with her." Tears welled, and Amity angrily brushed them away.

"I'll find him," Hank said, putting his arm around Amity. "And I'll give him a little hell if you want me to."

Amity laughed against his shoulder. "Yes, please." She pulled him close and placed a soft kiss on his cheek. "I'm sorry. And thank you."

"Nothing to be sorry for," he whispered in her ear. He strode out of the room, and Amity found that she still liked the view of him leaving.

AT 1:45 P.M., DR. FRENCH CAME BACK INTO THE WAITING ROOM. Amity had been half dozing, but she jumped up the moment she saw the doctor's familiar blue scrubs and kind eyes.

"Is Anne okay?" Amity said breathlessly, her hand over her heart.

"She is. And so is your new baby niece." Dr. French's eyes lit up with a smile.

Amity collapsed into the nearest chair, and this time she didn't try to stop the tears rushing from her eyes.

"Apparently just the *threat* of a Pitocin drip was enough to get things moving along." Dr. French laughed. "Delivery went smoothly. Everyone is in good health. Your niece is a perfect seven pounds, three ounces."

It took a moment for Amity to trust that she could speak. "Can I please see them?" she asked, her voice wavering.

"Now that the delivery is done, yes, we'll get you some scrubs and you can go back and see her."

Amity nodded her head vigorously. "I'd wear a space suit if you wanted me to."

Just then, a nurse walked in behind Dr. French with a stack of scrubs, and a mask perched on top. "Put these on over your clothes," the nurse mumbled behind her mask, "then use that hand sanitizer there." She waved at a black cube on the wall by the swinging door.

Dr. French returned to the maternity ward, but the nurse patiently waited for Amity to put on her scrubs. Amity dressed at warp speed, and the nurse led her back through the winding halls of the sprawling mountain hospital. Amity still found it a miracle that there was a hospital this close to St. Francis. When she arrived in Anne's tiny new hometown, she had assumed Anne would give birth in Aspen.

When the nurse opened the door to Anne's hospital room, Amity expected to be met with the sound of machines and the smell of antiseptic. What she encountered the moment her black boot crossed the threshold, however, was warm and welcoming. The room was a full suite with a picture window, a couch, and a rocking chair.

Anne was sitting up in the bed with a bundle of blankets in her arms and an empty bassinet next to her. She was flushed and appeared battle worn, with her hair mussed and her blue-and-white patterned gown askew. But she was smiling from ear to ear. "Want to meet your niece?" she whispered.

Amity rushed around to the opposite side of the bed from the bassinet. She hugged her sister's head tightly. "I was so worried," she whispered, her voice gravelly from hours of tension. She put her cheek against Anne's and looked down at the blanketed bundle for the first time—and fell in love.

The baby's tiny face was perfectly round, her cheeks perfectly rosy, and her eyes perfectly, peacefully closed. Amity had never seen anything so perfect in her life.

A buzzing in Amity's pocket snapped her to attention. "That must be Mark. Finally," she whispered. Pulling her phone out, she looked at the screen. It was a California area code.

Amity stared at the number.

"Is it Mark?" Anne asked, bouncing the baby in her arms.

"No," Amity answered.

"Are you going to answer it?"

"No." Amity put her phone back in her pocket. She knew exactly where she needed to be, now. And it wasn't L.A.

HANK

HANK HAD TO RUN FULL-OUT TO KEEP UP WITH MARK AS HE RAN across the hospital parking lot. He was half a step behind the man when Mark barreled through the sliding doors to the entrance and slammed his fists on the check-in counter.

"I need to get to the maternity ward," Mark demanded, wild-eyed, the shoulders of his trench coat rising and falling with each breath.

A security guard rose to his feet behind the young woman sitting at the desk behind a computer screen.

Hank put his hand on Mark's shoulder. "Let's calm down, man. I know you're anxious…"

"My wife is having a baby!" Mark didn't look at Hank, but continued to address the wide-eyed young woman at the computer. The security guard took a step forward, and Mark seemed to finally grasp what was happening. He took a steadying breath. "My wife's name is Anne Parish. I'm Mark Parish."

The woman nodded and typed something in. "I see you here. I'll print you a badge. Then take the elevators there," she motioned to the bank of elevators to Hank's right, "and go up to the fourth floor. There will be a welcome desk right when you step off the elevator, and they'll direct you from there." She handed Mark a printed sticker badge, and Hank could tell it was taking effort for Mark not to snatch it out of her hand and bolt with it.

When the men stepped off the elevator a few moments later, they entered the small waiting room and approached the desk on the other side. An older woman with short, curly gray hair sat behind bulletproof glass and looked up at them over her reading glasses.

"My wife is here," Mark said without waiting to be asked. "Anne Parish. I'm her husband, Mark." He pointed to the sticker on his starched purple button-down shirt.

The woman nodded and typed something on the keyboard in front of her. She pushed her glasses up on her nose to read the monitor perched on a stand to her right. "Mark. Gotcha right here. Seems Mrs. Parish has a guest in the room right now, and she's only allowed one guest. You'll have to wait…"

"Like hell I have to wait!" Mark said, his voice at fever pitch. He cleared his throat. "I'm sorry. I'm sorry."

Hank patted Mark's arm. "Let me call Amity and tell her we're here. I'm sure she'll come right out. Go sit down." He pushed Mark into a chair and gave an apologetic nod to the woman behind the glass.

It took four rings for Amity to pick up. "Hello?" she whispered hoarsely.

"We're here," Hank whispered back. *Why am I whispering?* "Mark is freaking out. Can you come out here so he can go back?"

"Coming," she said, then hung up.

After a minute, Amity opened the door. The moment she entered the room, Mark rushed back to the woman at the desk—but Hank's attention was fully on Amity. She was in black from her turtleneck to her pointed boots, but there was a happy flush to her face that made her style look romantic instead of severe.

Hank's neck was suddenly hot, and he pulled at the collar of his leather coat.

"What happened?" Amity asked as she took a seat next to Hank.

"He got a flat tire right on a stretch of I-70 with zero cell signal," Hank answered.

Amity rolled her eyes. "Of course. Let me guess. He was trying to surprise her by getting home earlier?"

"You know him well." Hank chuckled.

"Sadly." Amity's laughter ended in a sigh. "Anne gave birth not two hours after you left. No complications." She sighed again. "The baby is perfect." The emphasis on the last word signaled a joyful longing Hank had seen before.

"I'm so happy for you all," Hank said, and meant it. "When are you heading out?"

Amity cocked her head and gave Hank a confused look.

"Your flight to L.A.?" he reminded her with a smile. "Don't tell me that baby made you forget your big career move."

Amity looked at her hands. Her dark eyes rose slowly to meet his. "I'm not going."

"Not going today, or not going...ever?" he asked, surprised at the hope that was rising in his chest.

Amity shrugged. "I'm not sure what the future holds for me. But right now, I belong right here." Her face bloomed as her fuchsia lips stretched into a warm smile.

Hank put his hand on hers and squeezed. "Happy Christmas Eve."

Amity leaned over and placed a soft kiss on his lips. "Happy Christmas Eve," she whispered against his cheek.

Hank pulled Amity into a tight embrace and breathed in her jasmine scent. A thick blanket of pristine snow fell softly outside the waiting room window, turning the winter afternoon white. In that moment, Hank's world was quiet, peaceful, and whole.

AMITY

"A LITTLE HIGHER," AMITY YELLED UP AT HANK. HE HOISTED THE welcome sign up an inch, and she gave him a thumbs up. *He looks just as good from underneath as he looks from behind.*

Hank pounded a nail into the wall to hold the sign in place, then stepped down the ladder. "I still can't believe you made that in an hour." Hands on his hips, he looked up at the sign and shook his head.

Amity shrugged. "Artist," she said, pointing at herself.

"Yeah, but you make jewelry."

Amity squinted at him. "Jewelry is art."

"I'm not arguing that. But this sign is a thing of beauty, and it's not wearable."

Amity shook her head and decided to let this one go. The sign was some of her best *painted* work, for sure. Dozens of delicate roses encircled the words *Welcome home and Merry Christmas, Baby Rose!* and gold-flecked ivy weaved its way through the painted garden.

"I'm glad it turned out," Amity said, looking at her creation.

"I'm glad you still had the energy for it after last night," Hank said with a wink.

He put his arm around her, and for once, she didn't blush. For once, Amity felt at home—in this house, in this town, and in Hank's arms.

The sound of a car pulling into the graveled driveway made Amity jump. "They're home! They're early." She ran to the Christmas tree and quickly moved the pile of gifts covered in pink wrapping paper into a neat display, then rearranged a few ornaments so everything was perfect.

When Anne, Mark, and Baby Rose came through the door, Amity and Hank were holding hands under the painted welcome sign in the entryway. "Welcome home!" they yelled in unison.

"Look at this!" Anne said, pointing at the sign. She turned to her right to see the pile of presents, and pointed to that next. "And this! You two must have been at it all night."

This time, Amity did blush.

Mark walked around Anne with a covered baby carrier in one hand and a diaper bag in the other. "Thanks, you two." The new father was smiling from ear to ear, and his glasses were slightly askew.

"Oh, we're not done yet. There are scones in the kitchen, and there's a fresh pot of decaf coffee," Amity said proudly. "Decaf for you, right, Anne?"

Anne nodded, the fatigue evident in her brown eyes. "Sadly, yes. Decaf only while I'm nursing."

"Nursing," Amity whispered. "Wow. You're a mom." She went to her sister's side and pulled her into a warm embrace. "I'm so proud of you."

"I'm proud of you, too," Anne said softly. "It was a brave decision to not go to L.A. And I hope you know how happy I am that you'll be here to get to know your niece."

"I'm happy, too." Amity glanced back at Hank and grinned.

Hank leaned against the railing, out of the way. The Parish family walked by him and made their way to the kitchen, and

Amity grabbed his hand as she followed behind them, pulling him along.

Anne and Mark sat at the kitchen table with the baby carrier perched on a chair between them. They didn't wait for Anne and Hank before digging into the pile of scones.

"Thank you so much for making these," Anne said with her mouth full. "Hospital food is the worst."

"My pleasure," Amity said, leaning against the sink. As she surveyed the scene, she was overcome with a sense of gratitude for these people.

Hank stood in the center of the kitchen and rocked on his feet, his arms crossed. "I don't want to get anyone's hopes up… but I may have some good news."

All eyes turned to Hank.

He cleared his throat. "I discovered that it was Tricia who approved Donnelly's historical landmark application for the building Booktopia occupies."

Amity squinted.

"That's why I had dinner with her Friday night," he said, catching her look.

"You had dinner with Tricia Bonham?" Mark asked, incredulous. "Now that's taking a bullet."

Hank's smile was pinched. "I talked to my sister, Rebecca, the architect, about what I learned. She got me in touch with a tenants' attorney who is still working at the firm our dad retired from. The whole thing is fishy. The attorney and Rebecca both think that palms were greased, and the historical landmark status probably wouldn't hold up under scrutiny. Which means that the tax perks Donnelly has been enjoying wouldn't hold up, either."

Anne and Mark had stopped eating, and were staring at Hank with mouths agape.

"What does that mean?" Anne asked.

Amity noticed that Anne's hands were shaking, and she wondered if it was from excitement, hunger, or exhaustion.

"Nothing yet. But with an attorney looking into it now, if Tricia and her father are scamming the city...well, Donnelly is going to have a lot of back taxes to pay. Enough that maybe he has to sell that building. Quickly."

"And cheaply." Mark added with a nod.

"Cheap enough that maybe we could buy it?" Anne squeaked.

"Here's hoping," Hank said, smiling.

Amity pushed off the counter and wrapped her arms around Hank. "Thank you."

"Don't thank me yet..."

"Stop that," she said, playfully hitting his arm as she pulled back. "You keep saying that, but the fact is that you've been trying to help us all from the moment I met you. So let me say thank you." She kissed him softly, in full display of her sister and brother-in-law.

"It's a weekend of Christmas miracles," Anne said, pointing and laughing. She grabbed another scone and took a big bite.

Amity held Hank's hand, then turned to her sister. "You were right. I have a chance at a new kind of life, here. One that isn't driven by my career. I still have a lot to figure out...but I'm excited at the possibilities." She let go of Hank's hand, took a step over to the baby carrier, and pulled back the fleece cover. Rose cracked her eyes, then immediately went back to sleep. Amity sighed. When she looked up, Hank was staring at her with a bemused expression.

"They're hard to resist, aren't they," he said, stepping up and sneaking a peek of his own. "I hope you get to meet my nieces and nephews someday."

Amity's heart beat a little faster at that. She took Hank's hand again and gently pulled, bidding him to follow her out of the kitchen. She guided him to the front of the house, next to the glimmering Christmas tree. A soft snow was falling outside the window. She wrapped her arms around his neck, stroked his soft brown hair, and stared into his green eyes. He wrapped his arms around her waist and pulled her close. She nodded her chin toward the front door.

Hank's eyes went wide when he realized what she was pointing to. Hung neatly above the front door was a bright green sprig of mistletoe.

He pulled her in tight, and the passionate caress of his lips on hers sent her body aflame. She returned his kiss with equal enthusiasm. The world dropped away and for the moment, Amity's world was in Hank's arms.

Amity kissed her way to Hank's ear. "I'd love to meet your family someday," Amity whispered before kissing her way back to his lips. "But right now, I'm not going anywhere." Wrapped in his arms, with his body pressed against hers, Amity knew no gallery opening could match the joy of this moment.

PLEASE RATE AND REVIEW

We hope that you've enjoyed
A Rocky Mountain Romance
by Jessica Mehring.
Please consider leaving a review for this title.

Please rate and review : A Rocky Mountain Romance

MEET THE AUTHOR

Jessica Mehring is a Colorado-based author, copywriter and consultant. She believes that history and nature are our greatest teachers, yet she is also endlessly fascinated by technology and the human brain. She loves reading, walks in the woods, and creating and collecting art. She lives with her husband, two daughters, and more pets than she'd like to admit to — and her growing collection of books and office supplies are slowly taking over their house.

OTHER TITLES FROM

5 PRINCE PUBLISHING